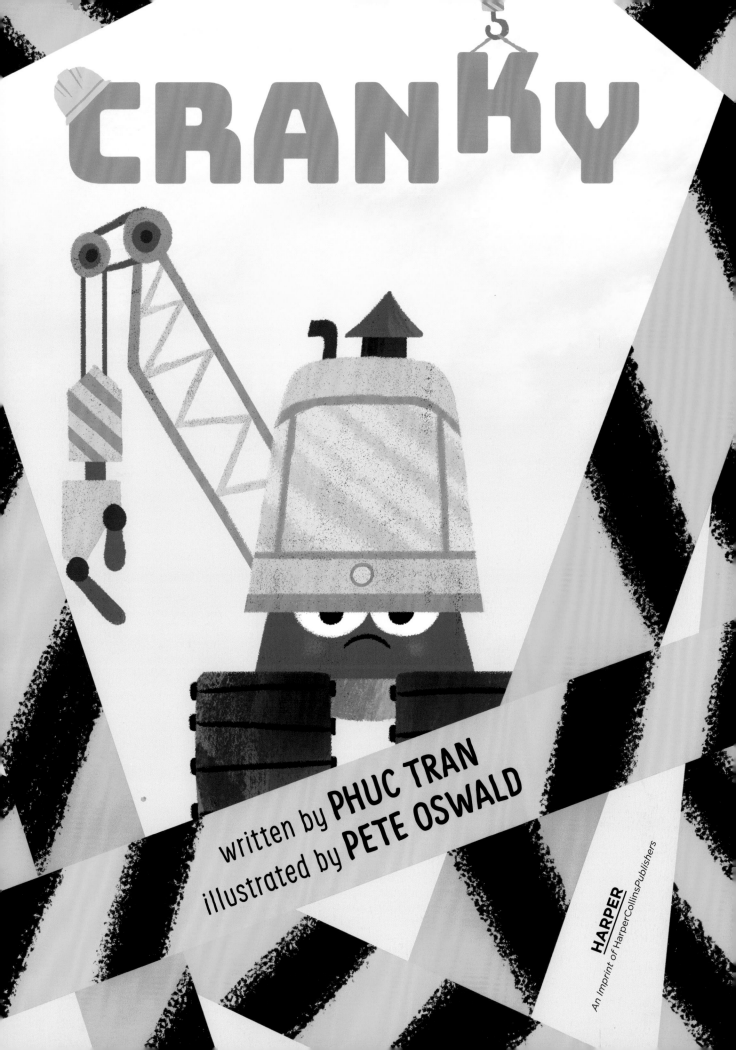

CRANKY

written by **PHUC TRAN**
illustrated by **PETE OSWALD**

HARPER
An Imprint of HarperCollinsPublishers

For Phoebe and Beatrix —P.T.

To Hank —P.O.

I'm Cranky.

And this morning I'm also *feeling* cranky because . . .

well, I'd rather not tell you. It's personal.

STOP

TAKE A HIKE

GO AWAY

BYE

No, my lug nuts are *not* too tight.

No, my clutch is *not* slipping.

I am a well-oiled machine,
thank you very much!

Just drop it. I said I don't want to talk about it.

It's our last day at the construction site and everyone is working really hard. Everything is shaking with crunching, hissing, and pinging as we rush to finish the bridge.

My friends Zippy, the cement mixer, and Wheezy, the forklift, sing out, "Good morning!" But I just grumble on by because I'm cranky. "Cheer up!" they insist, but this just makes me feel crankier.

You know what doesn't help when you're feeling cranky? People telling you to cheer up.

CRANKY

Dump Chuck needs help with the last beam, so I give him a hand.

At lunchtime, I *still* feel cranky.

I sit on one side of the bridge and see everyone else sitting on the opposite side.

I grumble over my can of beans, feeling even crankier.

You know what doesn't help when you're feeling cranky? Feeling left out.

It's time to put the last piece of the bridge into place.

Zippy, Wheezy, and the whole crew cheer as I hoist it up as high as I can. There's confetti and whistles and wheelies—we did it. We built the bridge!

I rumble away and sit by myself because I'm still feeling cranky, and now I'm tired, too.

You know what doesn't help when you're feeling cranky *and* tired? Happy people.

I watch the festivities. Jacques Hammer makes his famous crème brûlée, and there's a concert with our favorite band, Haulin' Notes. I hear the singing and laughter even from where I am.

Wheezy and Zippy come over.

Cranky, can we ask you something?

Maybe.

We noticed today that you are extra . . . cranky. Crankier than . . .

. . . your usual crankiness. Can you tell us what's wrong?

That! That *exactly*.

Zippy and Wheezy look like their wires are crossed.

What do you mean?

"There's *nothing wrong*. I just feel cranky and I don't want anyone to fix it and I don't want anyone to make me happy. And asking me what's wrong makes me feel like it's *not okay* for me to be cranky!"

I am suddenly roaring.
I may have blown my gasket.

Wheezy and Zippy idle quietly.

Can we say something?

Right now?!

My revving engine makes it too hard for me to hear
my friends. My self-of-steam needs time to cool down.

"No, guys. I'm too cranky to hear your words right now."

Zippy nods.

Wheezy and Zippy return to the party. I stay put and think about how my day went. It's the late afternoon now and I'm feeling the tiniest, teeniest, smallest bit *less* cranky (less gassy, anyway— I shouldn't have eaten so many beans for lunch).

On the radio, I call over to Wheezy and Zippy, and they meet me halfway—at the top of the bridge. It's beautiful.

My friends are giving me a lot to think about.

You know what *doesn't* make me cranky?

Knowing that my friends care about me . . .

even when I'm cranky.